Word of Mouth

Five Peculiar Short Stories

Harper Peters

ISBN: 9798488195790

DEDICATION

I dedicate this book to everyone.

THE HOROLOGIST

I met my neighbor Walter, an introverted horologist, outside my Boston apartment complex six months ago. I was sitting on a bench editing my book when he spoke to me for the first time. Wearing a button-down plaid collared shirt and dress slacks, he said, "I am stunned to see someone your age using a pencil instead of a phone." Although there were 30 years in age difference between us, he befriended me quickly. He seemed as interested in my work as a writer as I did in his clock-making. Neighbors saw him as an older man who avoided eye contact to deter small talk. To me, he was a fascinating human.

He told me exciting stories each Saturday while eating lunch together in his apartment. I listened to stories about his father, a horologist, who mastered his craft by twelve years of age. My favorite stories to listen to, though, were about his wife, Annabelle. Previously, he told me a touching story about how Annabelle's nebulizer suddenly stopped working during one of her routine usages. Everything from cleaning supplies to grass triggered her asthma, so she used an inhaler and a nebulizer as a preventative measure. While Walter removed the screws from the bottom of the machine to fix it, Annabelle sat calmly in a rocking chair, watching kids play hopscotch on the sidewalk through their apartment window. The children were laughing so loudly Walter and Annabelle could hear them in their apartment. The laughter was so contagious Annabelle started laughing uncontrollably, which triggered her asthma. Panicked, Annabelle couldn't find her inhaler. It took Walter 5 minutes to find the cause of the breathing machine malfunction, and the broken plastic part was about the same shape and size as one of his spare metal clock pieces. He scrambled around his workstation until finally finding the clock piece needed; however, it was difficult inserting the foreign part adequately into the machine. At the last minute, Walter maneuvered the substitute piece to fit perfectly. Walter plugged it into the wall outlet and turned on the device. He removed Annabelle's long grey hair from her sweaty face and placed the nebulizer mask over her nose and mouth. Within a few moments, she could breathe normally again.

When I ate lunch with Walter a month ago, he was reticent. As expected, the table was set for three people, even though Annabelle never ate with us. She rested with a humidifier and an air purifier pointed at her while sleeping in the bedroom. Walter and I sat at the dining table next to his worktable and a gothic grandfather clock made of walnut and oak. I told him I loved his grandfather clock because it makes me feel like I am playing a musical version of the game Simon. Instead of remembering the order of colored lights, I memorize the musical notes the clock plays every 15 minutes. Paperwork, tools, and labeled containers with little clock pieces cluttered his worktable. A wooden bowl filled with sandwiches, each consisting of one slice of meat and a bun, and a jar of pickled eggs occupied the center of the dining table. I politely declined a pickled egg when he offered one because there was an unpleasant odor from an unknown source in his apartment.

We sat in uncomfortable silence for 15 minutes. Walter propped his forehead up with his left hand, a mannerism he displayed when something was on his mind. Eventually, Walter asked me, "Do you remember the story I mentioned about when I fixed the breathing machine to save Annabelle from dying of laughter?" I nodded my head in agreement. Walter continued, "Well, something happened on Thursday; Annabelle and I were on the train holding hands. Our stop was getting close, so we stood up and waited for the subway doors to open. As they opened, I stepped onto the station platform. Annabelle followed, but not quickly enough, and the back of her black pea coat got caught in the door as it shut. A passenger inside the train tried to pry the door open with his cane as the subway moved. But the passenger lost his balance and fell on the dirty train floor. I tugged her coat with all my strength as Annabelle attempted to undo the buttons, but it would not budge from the door. The subway was moving too fast, dragging Annabelle's body 100 feet before falling onto the tracks. I jumped down to her from the station platform. Annabelle looked like a professional contortionist on the subway tracks, and I couldn't get the image of her twisted body out of my mind. I haven't told anyone else she died. Telling people would make her death real. I don't want her to be deceased." Speechless, I handed him a tissue and hugged him.

Then, we heard a knock at the door. Walter immediately stopped crying and wiped his tears from his wrinkled face. Walter whispered, "He is here for me. Find the key and take care of it, so he doesn't send me to a mental institution." Confused, I asked, "Take care of what?" A man unlocked the front door before Walter could answer me. "Dad, why didn't you open the door? It's time to go check out nursing facilities. Where is mom?" "Your mom is *resting*," replied Walter. The stranger said to me, "My name is Charles. Who are you?" Without making eye contact, I replied, "I am his neighbor, Annie."

After a quick spat, Charles agreed with Walter to tour nursing facilities. Walter felt fully capable of taking care of himself while Charles worried about his parents because they were aging. Before they left, Walter asked Charles if I could visit him when he moved. Charles agreed and handed me his business card, which read Charles Swan support group on the top of it. "Here is my business card. I have a corporate job, but I also run a grief support group. I learned how hard the grieving process was when I lost my son. So I created this weekly group to offer support to anyone going through a similar situation. Anyone grieving is welcome to attend. You can check out my website. We have excellent reviews. You can call me anytime to get in touch with Walter. Walter needs to stay in contact with his friends." I told him I was sorry for his loss and placed his business card in my purse.

We left Walters's apartment. I walked down the hallway to my place and sat on the couch, thinking about what Walter was trying to tell me. Then, I walked back to his apartment to look for clues after picking the lock to the front door. Once inside, I walked around the dining room and kitchen. A small wooden box on the kitchen counter fell onto the carpet, and a black and white picture of Walter and Annabelle on their wedding day fell out of it.

After opening all the kitchen cabinets and drawers, I felt discouraged about not finding a key. The gothic grandfather clock struck thirty minutes past five. It started playing a melody that reminded me the clock had a hidden compartment in the bottom front section. Walter showed me once how to open a secret cubby in it. I moved an attached statue of a boy to the right, which opened the hidden compartment like Walter once demonstrated for me. There it was. A tiny silver key sat in the cubby of the clock.

I looked around the apartment for things requiring a key to open. First, I checked the bedroom doorknob to see if Walter locked it. I twisted it, opened it, and walked into the bedroom. A perfectly made bed and recently dusted dresser made the room appear tidy. However, the bedroom smelled worse than the dining room. I grabbed a plaid hand towel from the bathroom and held it over my nose and mouth. The only space I had not checked was the closet. As I opened the closet door, I fell to my knees. I could barely breathe because of the horrid smell. After a few moments, I stood up and looked around the closet. A large black suitcase with wheels sat on the right side of the closet floor. Next to it, there was a pillow and a blanket. I sat on the blanket with my nose and mouth still covered by a towel.

To unzip the suitcase, I needed a key to a padlock. I pulled the key I found out of my pocket to see if it fit into the lock. I inserted the key. Once I twisted the key, the lock fell off the zipper holes. I started to unzip the suitcase, but the zipper was stuck on something long and gray. After yanking it, I pulled the long grey thread between the zipper and seam, and I unzipped the suitcase completely. Once I opened it, I discovered the grey thread was long, grey dirty hair. The bag held a twisted human body. The head was closest to the top of the suitcase. I moved grey hair away from the pale, lifeless face, and I confirmed it was, in fact, Annabelle. I rubbed my hands on my pants in disgust. I zipped up the suitcase, shut the closet door, and crawled to the bed in a panic. I started to think about everything Walter told me about Annabelle. He loved her deeply and more than anything else in the world. To know Walter loves her so much and could not part with her dead body and sleeps with her corpse at night in the closet is madness and insanity, but it is equally romantic.

Maybe he does need to be admitted to a mental hospital, I thought. But, if I could find the nebulizer, open it, and see a clock piece inside, I would believe Walter's stories about Annabelle and take care of the body as he wished.

So I searched his apartment for a nebulizer. I found it in a bathroom cabinet. I plugged it up to see if it would turn on. It worked. I opened the nebulizer with a screwdriver I found on his workstation. And there it was—an off-colored metal piece inside the device that didn't look like it belonged with all the other manufactured parts. Walter was not a killer, but his reputation was essential to him. He doesn't want a reputation for being insane.

I heard Walter and Charles enter the front door and walk into the dining room. Charles nagged at Walter for not locking the front door. Then, Charles told Walter he was going to check on his mom. Walter suggested he not wake up Annabelle, but Charles opened the bedroom door stubbornly. I quickly jumped in the bed and covered my face and body with blankets. Luckily, Charles didn't lift the covers. He padded my head through the blankets and said in a soft voice, "Get some rest, mom." The plan worked. He thought I was Annabelle. He left the bedroom and told Walter he would come back tomorrow to help them pack.

After Charles left, Walter walked inside the bedroom confused. He saw my body under the covers. He said, "Annabelle?" I uncovered my face. But, Walter was shocked at the sight of a body in his bed. He fell to the ground in emotional stress. He couldn't see my face from where he dropped to the floor because the bed blocked his view. He had an adrenaline rush thinking Annabelle had come back to life. I scared Walter to death.

Then, I heard the twisting of the closet doorknob. Lights in the apartment started to flicker on and off. A ghost with long grey hair and a black pea coat floated over to Walter's dead body, and Walter's spirit released from his body. Two ghosts hovered at the foot of the bed, holding hands as they stared at me. Walter's ghost blew me a kiss. Then the spirits flew out of the bedroom. I ran to the living room to follow them, but they had disappeared.

Before I called the police, I hid the black suitcase in my apartment. I went back to Walter's apartment and waited for the cops to arrive. When they got there, I told them Walter fell to the ground and stopped breathing. They said it looked like the death of natural causes, and they would contact me if they needed anything further. I provided them with Charles's phone number.

The only thing left for me to do was fulfill Walter's wish of disposing of the evidence. I buried her in the woods at a park.

RED LIPSTICK

Standing behind a podium, Elizabeth spoke to a small audience, "My husband, daughter, and I was in a traffic accident. After they died at the hospital, I fell into a deep depression and lost my job. While packing my things due to being evicted from my house, I found a pamphlet given to me by a nurse named Martha at the hospital for Charles Swan's support group. Martha told me this group helped her through the bereavement process. Once she started talking to people at the support group and listening to their stories, she started to feel better. So I decided to give the group a chance. Annie was the first person I met when I joined. She let me live with her and helped me find a job. I am thankful to Annie and all of you for listening to me. Thank you."

Elizabeth exited the stage and sat in an empty seat in the front row next to Annie. Elizabeth admired Annie for seeming so put together. Annie dresses business casual and wears red lipstick every day.

Charles Swan was the next speaker. He walked confidently to the podium. "Thanks, Elizabeth, for sharing your story with everyone," Charles said appreciatively. He smiled charmingly at Annie and Elizabeth as he moved his shoulder-length black wavy hair from his pale face with his hand. "Now, as you all know, the five stages of grief are anger, denial, bargaining, depression, and acceptance. Most people dealing with grief find the acceptance stage the hardest. But, which one of the five stages do you find the most difficult right now?" Charles looked around the room for raised hands. He points to Annie. Annie yells, "Anger." "The anger stage is difficult, Annie." Charles holds up a picture for the audience to see. He continues, "This is a picture of my mother, Annabelle. She has been missing for a month. I'm so angry with the police for not putting any effort into finding her. Anyone dealing with the anger stage of grief right now, I promise, we will make it through this together. I enjoyed seeing everyone tonight. I will see you next week."

Usually, Elizabeth and Annie left the weekly meeting together. But tonight, Annie is going with her friend Emily from Salem. Emily is driving Annie to her Salem house. Emily attends weekly meetings too, but Elizabeth has never met her.

As Elizabeth got into the car to drive to the apartment she shared with Annie in Boston, she saw Charles talking to Annie and an unknown woman in the parking lot. Charles handed them keys. Annie and the woman got into a black car. Elizabeth stopped by the liquor store to purchase four bottles of Merlot on the way home. But she didn't drink any of it because she had terrible anxiety. So, Elizabeth drove to the gym to work out. Maybe working out will help me feel better, she thought. After running on the treadmill for 30 minutes and lifting a few weights, Elizabeth left the gym. Working out was not helping her anxiety. As she walked out the front door, she looked across the street at a green and white-colored house. There was a light on inside. The resident had the curtains partially open, and she could see directly through the front bay window of the house. A woman wearing bright red lipstick was sitting on a couch.

Elizabeth drove back to the apartment. She looked in the rearview mirror touching the scar on her forehead from the car accident. After cleaning and reading, Elizabeth decided to drink some wine and watch a movie to help her sleep through the night. Tossing and turning in bed, she was too obsessed over the woman she saw in the bay window. Not many people can pull off bright red lipstick, she thought.

Curious, Elizabeth drove back to the house to get a better look at the woman. Parking the car a few blocks away from the gym and carrying a half-full bottle of Merlot, she walked the rest of the way. At 11 pm, the only light in the house was coming from a television. She spotted the mysterious woman talking on the phone through another crack in the curtain, but only the back of her head was visible. A rag and some kind of bottle with liquid in it sat on a brown dresser. An older man was sitting in a chair watching television. A neighbor's dog started to bark which got the woman's attention inside the house. The mysterious woman turned around and looked out the window. Elizabeth ducked down out of her view quickly.

As she walked the perimeter of the house, she passed by another bedroom window. She could see a man and a young girl sleeping. She pressed her nose and hands on the cold glass in an attempt to get a better look. But no matter how hard she pushed on the glass, she could not see them any better. The room was too dark. In her drunkenness, they looked like her deceased husband and daughter. She searched the house for an unlocked window to gain entry into the home. She finished the bottle of wine and threw it in the neighbor's trashcan. The dog stopped barking when Elizabeth crawled into a slightly open basement window. Finding her way into the kitchen, Elizabeth grabbed the first knife visible and stuck it in-between her sock and boot. Walking down the hallway, the first room she came to was door number 5. Elizabeth entered the room.

A bed with stained tan sheets was in the center of the room. Something in a sphere shape was under the sheets. Next to the bed, there was an assortment of knives. They were sitting on top of a nightstand next to a dim lamp. Hesitantly Elizabeth pulled the sheets down and uncovered the object. It was a decapitated female human head with blonde hair. Elizabeth whispered, "Buzzkill." The rest of the body was nowhere in sight. Elizabeth panicked and reached for her phone in the back pocket of her jeans to call the police. But she was too distraught and dropped her phone on the ground. She almost had a hold of it when someone came from behind her and pressed a rag against her mouth. A male voice said to her, "I see you've met my wife." Elizabeth wasn't powerful enough to free herself from her attacker. She fell to the floor. About 5 minutes passed before the chloroform wore off. When Elizabeth opened her eyes again, she heard people talking. It was Annie and Charles. Nauseous and disoriented, she closed her eyes so they wouldn't know she was awake yet. Annie said, "I can't do this. I can't kill them." Charles said sternly, "This will help us get through the anger stage of grief. I'm mad at you for killing my father. But, if you kill them, I will forgive you."

Then, it was silent. Elizabeth slowly crawled to the door and listened for voices. Elizabeth walked down the hallway to room number 6, hoping to find her husband and daughter there. As she walked into the room, a man and young girl were sleeping in a bed and tied up with a rope. Disappointment and acceptance came over Elizabeth from discovering they were not her husband or daughter.

Nonetheless, she felt the urge to save them, so she walked to the bed. As she walked towards them, she stepped on something crunchy. She looked down curiously and picked up something small, blue, and rectangular. It was a Tylenol PM tablet. She used the butcher knife from her boot to cut the rope. However, she couldn't wake or move the man or girl. So she crawled out the window to run to the gym for help. But before she could make it safely out the window, Charles ran into the room and grabbed one of her legs. But she kicked him in the face until she saw blood gushing down his lips. Once she broke his nose, he released his tight grip from her leg and let her free while he screamed in agony. Elizabeth ran across the street to the gym for help. A gym worker and Elizabeth were startled by the sound of one gunshot.

Annie ran out of the house to the gym and spotted Elizabeth. Annie told her Charles was dead. Elizabeth had a lot of questions. Annie told her she would tell her everything once the police came and they could go home. Annie said, "How did you know where I was?" Elizabeth responded, "Red lipstick."

CATCH-22

At the age of three, I found out my mother was a prostitute. Her pimp held me for ransom in his van while she worked the corner; opening the vehicle's side door, I saw her standing on the street corner waiting for a client. A tear rolled down her face as she mouthed to me everything was going to be okay. I shouted, "Mom, don't leave me." I like to think she cried tears of joy because I spoke a complete sentence for the first time that day. As I grew older, I thought money would make our life better. But when I met Theo in college, my thoughts about money changed forever.

Theo and I were the only students in French History class that wrote our class notes in a black and white composition notebook. Our professor told captivating French History stories instead of reciting facts from a textbook; I appreciated his teaching style. As long as I wrote and memorized his key points, I passed every exam. One night when class ended, I picked up a composition notebook from my desk. When I arrived home and sat down on the couch to complete my homework, I pulled out the notebook from my bookbag. But, the first page did not have any of my French History notes. No French History notes were in the notebook at all. The first page consisted of a bucket list. Theo's signature was at the bottom of the page, next to what appeared to be a bloody thumbprint with the initials IAN.

During the next French History class, I told Theo I took his notebook by mistake. He grabbed the notebook from my hands and asked if I had read it. Ashamed, I told him yes. Then, he asked me if I wanted to help him complete his list. I agreed to help as long as my bloody thumbprint wasn't required. He giggled.

His family went on vacations when he was a young boy, but once his parents started earning a lot of money, they stopped going on holidays. His parents were so busy with work that they were oblivious to his extreme loneliness and depression. But, when the maid told his parents she found Theo practicing tying rope knots to make a noose, his mother started taking him to therapy weekly. The therapist prescribed him Paxil.

The following weekend, he drove us to Wood Point amusement park in his luxury vehicle to complete the first task on the list of riding a wooden roller coaster. We arrived at Wood Point to ride the coaster named Mean Peak. It was the tallest and most unstable-looking wooden coaster I had ever seen. There was no wait in line, so we got in a cart quickly. As our cart moved down the tracks, we could feel every bump and turn. The wood made creaking noises as we rolled over the boards as if we were too heavy for the structure to hold us. Before we made it to the top of the highest peak, I felt like we were going to roll backward and plummet to our death. And, if we didn't fall, there seemed to be a good chance we would sever a body part before the ride was over if we didn't keep our arms inside the cart at all times.

Because it was a long drive home from the amusement park, I stayed the night at Theo's cold apartment. A presence that was the opposite of love surrounded us in his flat. Evil was following Theo, but I ignored my intuition, as girls sometimes do. Before we went to sleep, Theo said, "If you weren't with me, I would play Russian Roulette." Why would someone want to die, I thought.

He continued, "Sometimes I feel like I have blinders on, and I am walking in a dark tunnel. My peripheral vision is grey and blurry. The only option is to die inside the tunnel. But with you here, you make me laugh. You are funny." I was at a loss for words. He fell asleep. I was wearing a hooded sweatshirt and covered with a heavy bed comforter, but I could not get warm or forget the words he said to me before he fell asleep. I am a person that doesn't have my shit together. I can't even pick a major in college and stick with it, let alone be there for someone ready to off himself. I am not strong enough to be the person he needs. I'm terrified of being responsible for someone else. After 2 hours of lying in his bed staring at the ceiling, I finally fell asleep. I dreamt I was sleeping with him in bed, but someone was sleeping between us, and they reached their arm around me and covered my mouth with their hand. I woke up and sat up in bed abruptly. Theo woke up and grabbed his fully loaded handgun from the nightstand. I said I was startled by a weird dream. He set the gun down and went back to sleep, but I was awake for the rest of the night.

The following weekend he drove us to the lake to complete more of the bucket list tasks. On the way there, we stopped to use a restroom and eat at an Amish restaurant. Theo was embarrassed because his medication made him have diarrhea frequently. I told him, "Shit happens." While we ate, he told me he would kill himself if I weren't there with him. I could feel myself pulling away from him. I didn't know how to fix him. After finishing our food, we drove to the lake. We rented a jet ski and took turns driving it before we parasailed. Once we completed these two items on the list, he told me I was making all his dreams come true.

The following day, he called me to complete the final mission. At first, I told him I was too tired to go with him that night to the haunted building named The Millerhill Schoolhouse for Boys. But when I told him I wasn't going with him, he said he would probably kill himself. I immediately changed my mind. I didn't want his death to be on my conscience. I told him I would take a quick nap after work, and then I would meet him at his house for the final task.

He drove us from his house to The Millerhill Schoolhouse, where the principal killed 20 students in 1960. People say the students' souls are stuck there. The only thing he remembers about the school is his friend Ian. When he was younger, he went to school there, but his parents took him out in second grade because of the ghost rumors. About a week after he transferred to another school, Millerhill Schoolhouse closed permanently.

Thugs kicked in the front door of the school and shattered all the windows before we arrived. It was dark outside, and there was no electricity inside the brick building. Theo seemed more high-strung than usual. He turned on his flashlight and walked directly inside. First, we found the principal's office and noticed some dusty pictures hanging on the wall. In one of the pictures, it was a class from 1960. It was a black and white photo of kids posing in their uniforms. One of the students looked like the boy in my nightmare. I told Theo to look at the picture. When he looked at it, he said 1960 was the wrong year. His face turned white.

All of a sudden, we heard the song The Twist by Chubby Checker coming from the basement. Theo and I walked towards the basement. The old wooden floor creaked. Then, Theo fell through a hole, dropping his flashlight next to my feet. I shined the light through the hole, and I yelled his name, but he didn't respond. I walked down the stairs to the basement. Surprisingly, Theo was able to stand after the six-foot fall. The Twist started playing again on a dusty record player. The boy from my dream was standing behind Theo. I told Theo to turn around, and he saw the boy. He yelled, "Ian!" Ian had a rope, and he scooted a chair under a water pipe connected to the basement ceiling to reach it. Then, he hung a noose from the pipe. I ran over to Theo, but Ian pushed me away forcefully, and I slammed my head on the wall, fell to the ground, and blacked out.

I felt rodents crawling on me and nibbling on my bleeding head and I heard someone's voice. As I opened my eyes, I discovered it was Ian talking. He said, "With Theo's mental state, I knew he would be my best friend forever and come back to me."

Two rats were crawling on my stomach as I sat up. Then they quickly scattered behind old furniture. I stood up in a daze. Theo stood behind me as he covered my eyes with his hands and said, "I don't want you to remember me this way." He covered my eyes as we walked upstairs and out of the basement. But once I was outside, the apparition was gone.

I called the police anonymously to tell them about Theo in the basement. Then I searched the glove compartment of Theo's vehicle to find his parents' contact information to tell them what happened when the time was right. I walked to the first open gas station I found and called a taxi to take me home. That night, I found my passion, and it wasn't taking basic college classes.

THE APPLE DOESN'T FALL FAR FROM THE TREE

What place are people most vulnerable? I needed to answer this question before executing the perfect murder. People are unguarded at night while sleeping in their warm beds. However, I needed to murder my wife somewhere other than at our house, and I needed to make it look like she wasn't the target. I would be a person of interest to the police if I didn't.

My wife and I made a fortune from our corporate jobs to buy luxuries like sailboats and sports cars. We docked one of our sailboats at the Shangri-La marina. The name Shangri-La was fitting, considering people who live on boats feel they are in paradise. However, a weakness of free-spirited slip renters is they are too trusting. They form close relationships by fishing, swimming, drinking alcoholic beverages, and eating together. Any outsider who visits the marina with a free case of beer or food is welcome with open arms. Slip neighbors let their guard down. They sleep with boat hatches open to circulate ocean wind through the cabin. They don't worry about intruders.

Our son Theo committed suicide because of my wife. She took him to a doctor when our maid told us she caught him making a noose. They prescribed him Paxil, and he was taking it regularly, even though there were horrible side effects. Aside from being high strung, he had frequent bouts of nausea and diarrhea. But, his therapist pulled the wool over Nancy's eyes and insisted he was getting better on the medication. A college boy with a bright future didn't need a prescription. He should have come to me to talk about things. I would have taken time off work if I needed to so I could help him.

Before getting away with murder, I created a positive reputation. First, I formed Charles Swan's support group where people converse about deceased loved ones. I traveled to hospitals in the area, and I spoke to nurses about my support group. It took a lot of work, but now I have 50 loyal members attending weekly meetings.

Second, I needed someone to feel so guilty about something they have done that they would do something for me in return for forgiveness. Around the time I created the grief support group, I met my father's neighbor Annie, who scared him to death. Now, I don't believe she killed my father intentionally. Nonetheless, I made her feel like it was her fault to persuade her to assist me with my ultimate plan. So far, she listens to me like a puppy because she doesn't want me to think she is responsible for my father's death. My mother's death is what I hold in my back pocket if Annie decides to disobey me. I followed her to the park the night after my father's demise. I watched her dig a hole to bury a black suitcase with my mother's body inside of it until sunrise. Annie thinks I won't believe my father was insane if she keeps his secret. She tried to hide that my father held my mother's corpse in a suitcase for three days because he didn't want to part with her body. There is nothing she can do to change that the apple doesn't fall far from the tree. I went to my parents' apartment to check on them the day before I met Annie for the first time. They weren't home. Upon entering their bedroom, I found my mother's body twisted in a black suitcase on the bed. Seeing her dead body seemed like a test. If I could look at my mom and feel numb, I knew killing my wife would be a piece of cake. I didn't even cry. As I zipped the suitcase back up and walked into the dining room, my father came home from Lowes with a padlock.

When I visited my father the next day, Walter suspected I knew Annabelle was deceased. I acted normal to put his mind at ease.

Walter and I had gone to look at nursing facilities. When we returned, I told my dad I would check on my mom in the bedroom to mess with him. He didn't want me to go to the bedroom and see that she was not there. However, Annie did surprise me by lying in my dad's bed to pretend to be Annabelle. I saw Annie under the blankets. I knew it was not my mom because I saw a few strands of Annie's uncovered brown hair. The loyalty Annie possesses is something I would use to my advantage soon.

Third, I fought with my wife on purpose every night after work in an attempt to make her leave the house and live on our sailboat. I recommended she live on the boat; after all, we named the boat after her. I spent hours each night saying horrible things to Nancy. I told her she was getting old and fat; she was the cause of all my problems. After 30 years of marriage, I knew all the right buttons to push to get under her skin. What rattled her most was when I told her not to talk, and I knew everything. If I was exhausted hearing myself talk, I can't imagine how exhausted she must have felt. Although I have to commend Nancy on holding her composure, everyone has limits. After a week of verbal torture, she packed her necessities and went to live on our sailboat.

During the week before the mission, Annie went to the marina to collect information about the people living there. She picked people we could easily overpower. I can see why my reclusive father liked her so much. She had an eye for detail. She was able to gather a list of victims quickly. We planned to murder them all on the same night. The first victim is Henry, a 60-year-old male with a bad leg. He injured his right leg during a boating accident, so he uses crutches to help him walk on days when he's in pain, typically when a storm is approaching. The second and third victims were a man named Lee and his daughter named Mindy. He was an easy target considering his daughter was all he had left after his wife died of cancer. A drunkard spends most of his days on the dock listening to Jimmy Buffet until he falls asleep. He is killing himself slowly with alcohol, and we would be doing him a favor. Mindy is a nine-year-old girl in the wrong place at the wrong time. The last victim is, of course, my wife, Nancy.

Shortly after I met Annie, I met a young woman named Emily. She attended one of the weekly meetings and introduced herself to me. She told me she was the last person who saw Theo alive. She called the police when she found him hanging from a water pipe in the basement of Millerhill Schoolhouse for Boys. I trusted Emily more than Annie, probably because she knew my son. One night after a meeting, I told Emily how I felt Nancy was the cause of Theo's suicide, and I wanted revenge. Emily's willingness to assist Annie and me was surprising. Emily rented a house in Salem to take the victims and dispose of all evidence.

After the support group meeting this week, I gave Emily and Annie the keys to the rooms for the victims. Strong locks were installed on the bedroom doors so there would be no escapes. When I arrived at the house at 11 pm, Annie and Emily were already back from the marina. Emily told me there was a problem with Nancy, so she had to kill her before I got there. I went into room number 5. Sure enough, Nancy was dead. Her bloody head sat on a bed in the middle of the room. However, her body was missing. Emily told me she had no problem taking care of Nancy because it is what Theo wanted.

Henry was in room number 4 watching television. The girls had told him he would stay at their house for a few days while they cleaned his sailboat, so he stayed willingly. Then, I walked to room number 5 because I heard a noise, and I found Elizabeth. Without thinking, I came from behind Elizabeth while she bent down searching for her phone on the ground. I held a chloroform rag to her mouth and nose. She fell asleep, and her limp body fell on the carpet. I told Annie she needed to take care of the rest of the victims now, but Annie had cold feet. Eventually, I persuaded her to continue with the plan, and we left Elizabeth sleeping while we went to Henry's room. He was the easiest victim to kill. Annie unlocked Henry's room door. But, I heard a noise again. It sounded like it was coming from room number 6. I walked into the room and found Elizabeth had cut the rope used to restrain Lee and Mindy, but they were still sleeping. Elizabeth was trying to escape out a bedroom window, so I grabbed her leg. But she kicked me in the face and broke my nose. I ran into the hallway. I yelled at Annie and told her she needed to stop procrastinating and kill the rest of the victims, and if she didn't do it this instant, I would call the police and tell them where she buried my mother's body in the park. Annie was stunned. She didn't move. Emily pulled out a gun and attempted to shot me in the head but missed. I started choking Emily but stopped when I felt something sharp enter my back. At first I felt warm blood on my face and arms when I fell to the floor. But now I feel nothing. I feel nothing like when I saw my mom's dead body in a suitcase.

THE LETTER

Dear Lily,

How is my sweetest granddaughter doing in your new high school? I bet you are doing great. Have you decided on a costume for Halloween? This year, I am dressing up like Captain Ahab from your favorite book. Nancy, Lee, and Mindy are dressing up as characters from your favorite book too! They told me to tell you they have missed you since you moved from the marina to Tennessee. Many unbelievable things have happened here.

I met two women named Annie and Emily at the marina. You would like them if you were still here. Each day, they visit me to check on my bad leg. They also bring me chicken wings to eat and Stella Artois to drink.

Emily reminds me of you in some ways. She learns things from watching YouTube videos as you do. Emily is learning how to do special effects gore makeup from watching videos on her Smartphone. She has been practicing special effects makeup on my bad leg. She will make my leg look like part of it is missing from a whale attack for my Halloween costume. When I found out she didn't scare easily, I showed her my feet and asked her to cut my toenails. You know I can't reach my feet anymore. It took her two hours, but she clipped and filed my toenails. I gave Emily $20.00 for being so kind.

I don't know if you ever met Charles Swan. He was Nancy's husband. Annie and Emily attend Charles Swan's grief support group weekly. Annie's friend and neighbor, named Walter, died, and he was Charles's father. Emily's friend Theo died from suicide, and he was Charles Swan's son.

Annie discovered the support group from charming Charles Swan himself. She met him right before Walter died. He sold Annie on the benefits of going to the meetings so well that she immediately started attending as soon as Walter died.

Emily felt guilty about Theo committing suicide. She thought she could have done more to help him. Emily researched Charles and Nancy online and found the Charles Swan support group website. One night, she stood on the sidewalk watching people leave a meeting. She saw Annie and introduced herself. Annie only had good things to say about the group. Emily decided to join. When she introduced herself to Charles, he immediately took a liking to her.

Charles expressed to Annie and Emily how he despised his wife because their son died; he wanted to slaughter Nancy but make it look like she was not the target. To do this, he planned to bring Nancy, Lee, Mindy, and me from the marina to a house Emily rented in Salem. Then Annie, Emily, and Charles were to kill us on the same night.

Annie and Emily are good people. Sometimes good people can deceive the most insane people. They went along with Charles's plan. But, there was something Charles didn't know. The girls clued us in on his agenda. Once I found out what he was planning, I carved new wooden crutches for myself.

On the day of the last weekly meeting, Emily came to the marina. She told us it was showtime. Emily completed most of Nancy's makeup in the cabin of her sailboat. Then Emily left and came back with Annie after the meeting a few hours later. They drove us to the Salem house to set up the *scene* before Charles arrived.

Emily unlocked my room. It was room number 4. The plan was to sit in the chair and watch television until it was safe to leave. Charles thought Annie and Emily told me they would clean my sailboat, and I could stay at the house until they finished cleaning it.

Annie took Lee and Mindy to room number 5. Lee dropped a few Tylenol PM on the floor and set the bottle on a nightstand by the bed to make it look like Annie and Emily gave them sleeping pills. Annie tied a rope around Lee and Mindy that was attached to a bed frame so they couldn't move.

Lastly, Emily and Nancy went into room number 6. Emily cut a hole in a mattress that was wide and round enough for Nancy's head to fit in it. Then, Nancy placed her head through the hole. Her head was sticking out of the top of the mattress. Nancy hid her body under the bed frame.

Emily used special effects makeup around the hole's perimeter to make it look like Nancy's head was chopped off and sitting on the bed. She dimly lit the room with an old lamp. She placed different knives with fake blood on them on a nightstand next to the bed.

The only rule was to stay in character no matter what. Everything was going according to plan.

When Charles arrived later that night, Emily told him she had to kill Nancy before he got there because she was getting mouthy. Charles went into her room, and he was delighted to see Nancy decapitated.

Something unexpected happened that night, though. Someone else from the meeting showed up, Elizabeth. She didn't know everything was a hoax. Charles tried to kill her in room 5 when she was trying to escape out of a window. I heard screaming. Something wasn't right. I knew I wasn't supposed to leave my room, but I didn't want the girls to get hurt. So I grabbed one of my crutches, removed the rubber stopper from the bottom, and went into the hallway where Charles, Annie, and Emily were. Elizabeth had kicked Charles in the face and broke his nose. He was a bloody mess. He yelled at Annie, "Kill everyone now!" Annie started to cry. He continued, "If you don't kill them now, I will tell the police where you buried my mom."

Emily pulled out a gun from her back pocket and attempted to shoot Charles. But she had a horrible aim. Charles started choking Emily. He yelled, "Now you get to feel the same neck pain as Theo!" Emily dropped the gun. Then, I stabbed Charles in the back with the bottom end of my crutch that I carved into a wooden stake. The stake was so sharp it went all the way through his back and stomach. He let go of Emily's neck. I pulled the stake out. He fell to the floor, dead. I was standing in a puddle of his blood. When the police arrived, we told them everything. The police deemed it as an act of self-defense. So that is all that has happened since you have left. I love you! Happy Halloween if I don't hear from you by then.

Love,
Grandpa

ABOUT THE AUTHOR

Harper Peters grew up in the United States on the east coast. She plans to write books until her imagination retires.

BOOKS

A Life in Poems
The Poetry of an Escapist
My Heart is Still Beating
Word of Mouth

Share book reviews on Goodreads.com

Follow Harper Peters on her Amazon author page to learn about new releases.

Website: Harper-Peters.com

Made in the USA
Columbia, SC
03 November 2021

48300514R00021